One night, he couldn't
sleep. It was a very
noisy, stormy night.

In the morning, Henry opened
his porthole and looked out.

The stormy night had turned
into a lovely, sunny morning.

But what was that noise?
Someone was crying.

From high up in the lighthouse,
Henry couldn't see who it was.

Grabbing his cap, he scampered
down the stairs to find out.

L

Henry lived in a lighthouse and helped the lighthouse keeper.

Hiding under piles of seaweed
was a tiny baby seal.

"What's the matter?" asked Henry.

"I was washed up here by the storm," cried Baby Seal. "I'm very hungry and scared. I want to go home."

What would Baby Seal eat?
Henry tried his favourite foods.

Cheese...

Cake...

Chocolate…

Baby Seal didn't like any of them and just cried louder.

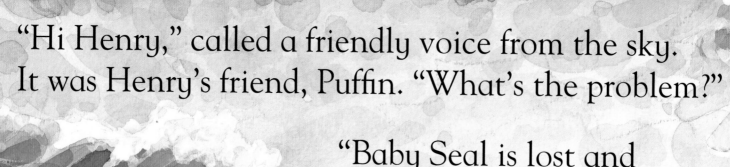

"Hi Henry," called a friendly voice from the sky.
It was Henry's friend, Puffin. "What's the problem?"

"Baby Seal is lost and
hungry and I don't know
what to do," said Henry.

Puffin smiled – he knew. He flew off
and soon came back with a big fish.

Baby Seal gobbled it up and stopped crying. Then they all agreed to search for Baby Seal's mother.

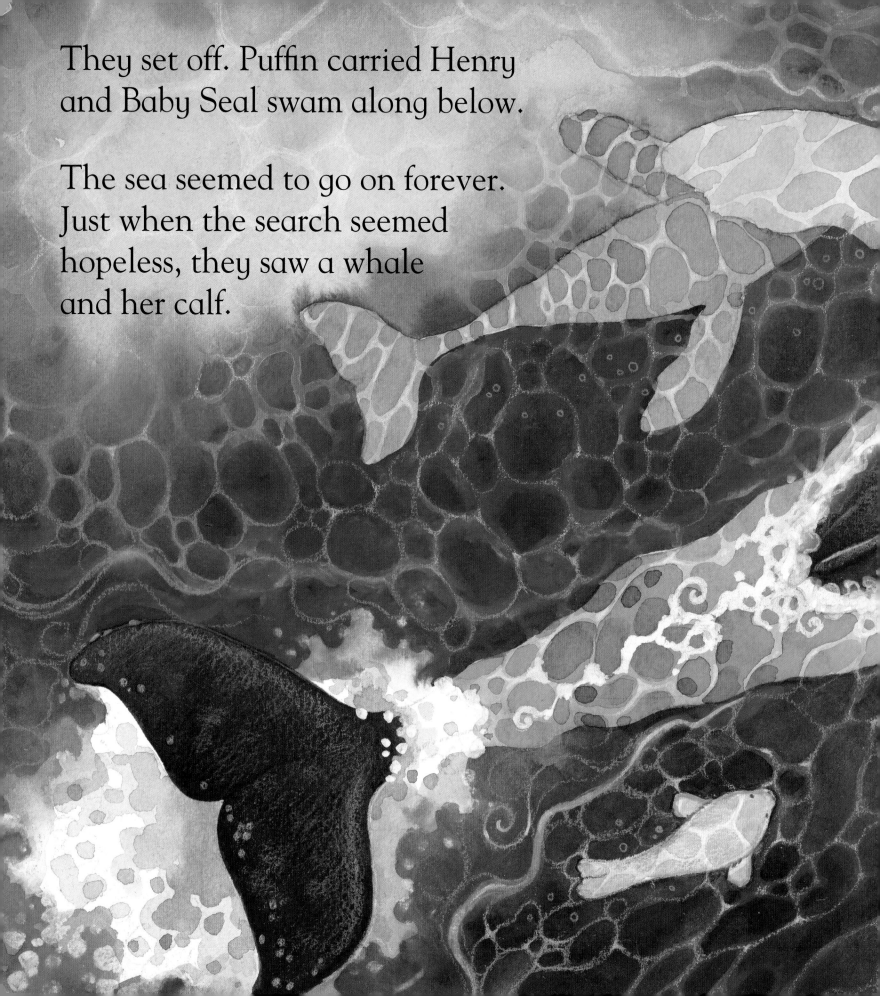

They set off. Puffin carried Henry
and Baby Seal swam along below.

The sea seemed to go on forever.
Just when the search seemed
hopeless, they saw a whale
and her calf.

"Baby Seal got lost in the storm," explained Henry. "We are looking for her mother. Have you seen her?"

"No, sorry," puffed Whale. "Have you asked Albatross?"

Soon they found Albatross.
"I've flown hundreds of miles
over the sea. I've seen ships,
islands and icebergs, but
I haven't seen Baby
Seal's mother."

"Ask Turtle," he called.
"He's usually swimming
around here."

Turtle was sad to hear about
lost Baby Seal.

"Sorry, I can't help," he spluttered. "I missed the storm. We were following the jellyfish from warmer seas. I did meet some dolphins who'd been in the storm. You could ask them."

Henry was fed up. They had
searched all day and hadn't
found Baby Seal's mother.
They were very tired. As the
sun began to set, they sat
on a buoy for a rest.

"You all look a little sad," called a friendly voice. "What's wrong?" Henry told Dolphin about lost Baby Seal. "I've seen Baby Seal's mother!" Dolphin cried.

Henry, Puffin and Baby Seal followed
Dolphin all the way back to the coast.
There on the rocks were some seals.

"Can you see her? Is she
there?" asked Henry.
Baby Seal shook her head.

They moved a little closer. "How about now?" Henry asked. Baby Seal shook her head again.

Baby Seal didn't see her mother, but her mother saw her.

She raced over to give Henry
and Baby Seal a big hug.
"Thank you for bringing my
baby back!" cried Mother Seal.

Back at home in the lighthouse, Henry had no trouble sleeping that night... no trouble at all.

Notes for parents and teachers

- Before starting to share this story with children, look at the front cover and help them to read the title. Can the children guess what the story is about and where it takes place?

- Henry lives in a lighthouse. Do the children know what a lighthouse is and what it is for? Explain what lighthouses do and where they are built. Have any of the children seen a lighthouse? The light can only be seen at night and when there is a thick fog. There is also a loud fog horn to warn the ships. What do the children think a fog horn would sound like?

- When Henry finds Baby Seal, he doesn't know what she eats. His friend Puffin knows. What did Puffin bring for Baby Seal? Is there anything else she might like to eat?

- Henry and Puffin meet a whale, dolphin and turtle in the sea. Can the children think of other creatures that live in the water?

- Ask the children to draw pictures, using the pictures in the book to help them, of a whale, turtle and smiling dolphin. Do dolphins really smile, or do they just look like it?

- Do the children know how big an albatross is and how far it can fly? What does it eat and where does it build a nest for its eggs?

- Ask the children to make a play of the story. Some of them can be Henry, Puffin and Baby Seal. Others can be the other characters in the story. What would they talk about and what sort of voices would they have?

- Seals live in the sea, but they can also come out onto the land. Can seals breathe underwater? Discuss how they keep warm in very cold water and how the mothers look after their babies.

- In the story, Baby Seal gets lost in the storm. Happily she finds her mother again with the help of Henry and Puffin. How do the children think it would feel to be lost? Would they know what to do it they got lost?

- Henry and Puffin are good friends and like helping anyone in trouble. Ask the children to talk about their friends. Can they think of a time when they helped someone? What did they do and how did they feel?

Copyright © QED Publishing 2009

First published in the UK in 2009 by
QED Publishing
A Quarto Group Company
226 City Road
London ECIV 2TT

www.qed-publishing.co.uk

ISBN 978 1 84835 238 4

Printed and bound in China

Author Heidi Howarth
Illustrator Daniel Howarth
Designer Alix Wood
Project Editor Heather Amery

Publisher Steve Evans
Creative Director Zeta Davies
Managing Editor Amanda Askew